IT'S MY BIRTHDAY

Heidi Goennel

Tambourine Books

New York

Copyright © 1992 by Heidi Goennel
All rights reserved. No part of this book may be reproduced
or utilized in any form or by any means, electronic or
mechanical, including photocopying, recording, or by any
information storage or retrieval system, without
permission in writing from the Publisher.
Inquiries should be addressed to Tambourine Books,
a division of William Morrow & Company, Inc.,
1350 Avenue of the Americas, New York, New York 10019.
Printed in Hong Kong

The full-color illustrations were painted in acrylic on canvas.

Library of Congress Cataloging in Publication Data
Goennel, Heidi.   It's my birthday/Heidi Goennel.—1st ed.
p.   cm.
Summary: A child celebrates a birthday with a party,
long-distance telephone call, special card, cake, and gifts.
ISBN 0-688-11421-0 (trade.)—ISBN 0-688-11422-9 (lib. bdg.)
[1. Birthdays—Fiction.] I. Title.
PZ7.G554It   1992   [E]—dc20   91-30231   CIP   AC

1   3   5   7   9   10   8   6   4   2
First Edition

For my
mother and
father.

Guess what today is.

It's not the Fourth of July.

It's not Halloween.

It's my birthday. Now I'm a whole year older.

I just got a card from my friend Petey.
He lives far away now.

Nana has knitted a soft, new sweater for me. Uh oh.

Mommy and Daddy surprise me with a new bicycle. WOW!

All my friends come to my party.

We play lots of games,

we go on pony rides,

and we dress up as pirates to hunt for
hidden treasure.

We watch a magician pull a real rabbit out
of his hat.

Then we have ice cream and cake.
I make a big wish and blow out all the
candles. Happy Birthday!